This book belongs to

....

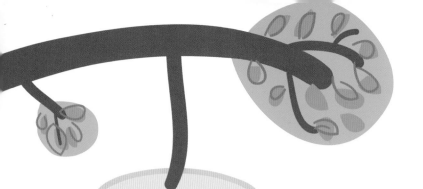

All Peppa Pig books are printed on paper from responsibly managed sources. This Peppa Pig book is printed with environmentally friendly vegetable inks and a water-based finish on the cover.

LADYBIRD BOOKS
UK | USA | Canada | Ireland | Australia | India | New Zealand | South Africa
Ladybird Books is part of the Penguin Random House group of companies
whose addresses can be found at global.penguinrandomhouse.com.

www.penguin.co.uk   www.puffin.co.uk   www.ladybird.co.uk

Penguin
Random House
UK

First published 2020
002

eOne   ASTLEY · BAKER · DAVIES ·

Printed in China

A CIP catalogue record for this book is available from the British Library

ISBN: 978-0-241-43672-1

All correspondence to:
Ladybird Books
Penguin Random House Children's
One Embassy Gardens, New Union Square
5 Nine Elms Lane, London SW8 5DA

FSC
www.fsc.org

MIX
Paper from
responsible sources
FSC® C018179

Peppa Loves Our Planet

It was Love Our Planet Week at playgroup.
Peppa and her friends were very excited.
"Welcome, children," said Madame Gazelle, pointing to a
picture of the world. "This is Earth . . . the planet we live on!"
"Wow!" gasped the children.

"The little things we do to look after our planet can make a big difference," continued Madame Gazelle. "Can anybody think of some things we can do to help?"

"Recycle!"
cried Peppa.

"Use less water!"
said Pedro Pony.

"Grow our own snacks!"
squeaked Rebecca Rabbit.

Crunch!

"Walk, not drive!"
said Zoe Zebra.

"Save electricity!" barked
Danny Dog, switching
off the lights.

Click!

"All **excellent** ideas!" said Madame Gazelle. "Well done.
But let's turn the lights back on for now, Danny, so we can see."
"OK," said Danny.

"Now, children, I'd like you each to make a Love Our Planet Scrapbook at home," said Madame Gazelle. "You can fill it with all the things you do to help look after our planet, and then bring it in for show-and-tell."

"Ooooh," gasped Peppa and her friends excitedly.
They loved making scrapbooks and they loved show-and-tell!

At home time, Daddy Pig arrived with Peppa and George's scooters. "Can we scooter home every day, Daddy?" asked Peppa. "It will be better for our planet if we don't use the car."

"Great idea, Peppa," said Daddy Pig. "I love scootering!"

Daddy Pig raced off, and Peppa
and George scootered after him.
"Wait for us, Daddy!" cried Peppa.

When they got home, Peppa and George helped Mummy and Daddy Pig with dinner. "If we put the peelings in the food-waste bin, Grandpa can use the compost on his garden," said Peppa. "Then he can help look after our planet, too."

"Lovely idea, Peppa," said Mummy Pig.
"We can take them to Grandpa tomorrow."

The next day, Peppa and George scootered over to Granny and Grandpa Pig's house with the food-waste bin.

"Thank you, Peppa," said Grandpa Pig, thrilled with his gift.
"Over time, these peelings will turn into compost, which will be
fantastic food for my plants and will help my garden grow very nicely."
"And it will help look after our planet!" said Peppa.

Then Grandpa Pig had a surprise. He gave Peppa and George
a window box to take home!
"These flowers are very important," he explained. "Bees and
butterflies love them! We need insects to help plants make seeds."

"Thank you, Grandpa!" cried Peppa,
buzzing around and pretending to be a bee.
"I'm a busy bee looking after our planet!"
"Buzz, buzz!" George giggled.

When they arrived home from Granny and Grandpa Pig's house, Peppa and George watered their lovely new window box.

"Look, George!" cried Peppa. "All these bees and butterflies have come to visit our new flowers. We're looking after our planet!"

After lunch, it was time to pop to the shops. "Daddy, remember to bring some old shopping bags so we don't have to get new ones," said Peppa.

"Great idea, Peppa," said Daddy Pig, picking up
some shopping bags to reuse. "Right, let's go!"

Just as they were leaving, George
pointed to the light switch.
"He wants to turn off the light to
look after our planet," explained Peppa.

"Thank you, George,"
said Mummy Pig. "I'll do it
for you. From now on, your
job can be to remind us to
turn off the lights."
George grinned. He was
very happy with his
new job!

That evening, Peppa and George tidied up and put everything into the right recycling bins.
"Let's sing the recycling song!" said Peppa.

"Recycle, recycle, we're going to recycle,

Tin cans . . . bottles . . . newspapers,

Recycle, recycle, we're going to recycle!"

"We'll take everything to Mr Bull's recycling depot tomorrow," said Mummy Pig. "But there's still **one** more thing left for us to do today . . ."

"Our scrapbooks!" cheered Peppa.
Peppa and George used some of the cardboard from
the recycling bin to make their Love Our Planet
Scrapbooks. Then they drew and stuck in pictures of
all the different things they had done to help look
after our planet.

"Wow, what lovely scrapbooks," said Daddy Pig. "They're recycled, Daddy!" said Peppa proudly.

At bedtime, Daddy Pig was the last one to brush his teeth.
"Make sure you turn off the tap while you're brushing, Daddy,"
said Peppa. "That way you won't waste any water."

"Splanks, Spleppa," mumbled Daddy Pig through a mouthful of toothpaste.

The next morning at playgroup, Peppa, George and their friends
showed Madame Gazelle their Love Our Planet Scrapbooks.

"Fantastic work, children!" said Madame Gazelle. "You've found lots of ways to look after our planet. I hope you've all learned that, when it comes to looking after our planet, every little thing makes . . ."

"...a BIG difference!" shouted Peppa and her friends, finishing Madame Gazelle's sentence for her.

Peppa, George and their friends love our planet!
Everyone loves our planet!